Toy Store
Trouble

READ MORE ADVENTURES ABOUT TWIG AND TURTLE!

TWIG AND TURTLE

Toy Store
Trouble

Jennifer Richard Jacobson

Illustrated by Paula Franco

PIXEL✛INK

For HJJ

PIXEL✚INK

Text copyright © 2020 by Jennifer Richard Jacobson
Illustrations copyright © 2020 by TGM Development Corp.
All rights reserved
Pixel+Ink is a division of TGM Development Corp.
Printed and bound in August 2020 at Maple Press, York, PA, U.S.A.
Cover and interior design by Georgia Morrissey
www.pixelandinkbooks.com
Library of Congress Control Number: 2020938108
Hardcover ISBN 978-1-64595-024-0
Paperback ISBN 978-1-64595-025-7
eBook ISBN 978-1-64595-052-3
First Edition
1 3 5 7 9 10 8 6 4 2

CHAPTER 1

"Where are all the spoons?" Dad asks.

"We have them," I say. It's Saturday. My younger sister, Turtle, and I are sitting on the floor of our tiny house, playing Magic Woods.

"All of them?" Dad asks.

"The evil spoons are invading our land, Daddy!" Turtle says. She marches her plastic elephant over to one of my baby skunks. "Hop on my back! I'll save you!"

Dad comes and peeks over the couch cushions

1

we set up as walls. "Hmmm. Who's the leader of this magic kingdom?"

"Queen Skunk," I say, making Mama Skunk peek out from her cave. She's fragile and the tip of her tail broke off one time.

Dad leans over. "Oh, Smelly One. Please command one captured spoon to retreat to Kitchen Land so I can make lunch."

"Not smelly!" I say, but I have Mama Skunk do as he asks. "Long Handle," I say in my queenliest voice. "You are banished. You must return home." I hand the spoon to Dad.

"What's for lunch?" Turtle asks, hopping up.

She abandons our game and heads for the kitchen end of the room to help make pesto pasta. (Which really means she leaves to do taste tests.) I don't mind. I like playing with my family of skunks in a little corner of the kingdom. I can make them talk in my head instead of out loud.

Turtle and I could only bring five toys each when

we moved to our tiny house. That's all that could fit in the small sleeping loft we share. (Mom and Dad also

3

have a loft across from ours.)

Winky, her elephant, and my porcelain skunk family are our favorite toys for this game. Here's how you play Magic Woods in a tiny house with only a few toys:

- Pull the rug into the middle of the room.
- Set up couch-cushion walls.
- Toss whatever dirty laundry you have inside the walls.
- Mold hills and paths and caves from the laundry.
- Find objects around the house to use as the other villagers and enemies.
- Save the kingdom from all sorts of disasters.

Dad tells us to pick up the game before we eat on the front porch (sunshiny day!). Then we can head to the library right after.

The hardest thing about living in a tiny house is

4

having to pick up. All. The. Time.

"Come help, Turtle," I say. The only time Turtle is actually pokey like a turtle is when there's picking up to do.

She meanders back, scoops up the dirty laundry, and carries it back to the hamper in the bathroom.

❧

Cara's Carrots Food Truck is right next door. As we pass by on our way to the library after lunch, Cara pokes her head out the window and sings, "I have carrot cupcakes today!"

Turtle and I look at Dad with raised eyebrows and our sparkliest *Please, please, please* eyes.

"Maybe on the way back," he says. He's eager to pick up a new book on the history of comics that the library got especially for him. Making comics is Dad's job.

"But we'll have armloads of books," I remind him.

"And we won't want to get them sticky from the frosting."

"Good thinking, Twig!" Turtle says to me.

Dad lifts one hand and rubs this thumb and pointer finger together. He always does that when he's making up his mind. Then he smiles and shrugs.

"Hooray!" Turtle and I cheer.

I knew my dad would give in. He's a cupcake guy. While we were eating our pasta earlier, we saw a long line forming at Cara's. But now that the lunch-time rush is over, we're the only ones here. Cara comes out and sits at the wobbly picnic table with us.

"I heard that the old bank building has been sold," she tells Dad.

"Does that make you sad?" he asks.

We knew that Cara had been trying to buy that building to open up a restaurant, but she didn't have enough money.

She shakes her head. "I'm not sure a restaurant would be as much fun as a food truck. It's a lot of hours."

"And a lot of cleaning up!" Turtle says.

Dad and I laugh. So does someone else.

"Mom!" I say. My mother is a photographer, and she's back from her meeting with a couple who are getting married. She takes pictures of us eating our cup-cakes.

The cupcake tastes like a warm rainbow with fluffy clouds on top, and I tell Cara that.

"Thank you, Miss Twig," she says to me. "If you want to come by sometime when it's not busy, I'll teach you how to make them."

"Really?" That reminds me. "Can I draw a cup-cake on your blackboard?" I ask.

"Of course!" she says. "Go ahead and get the chalk."

Turtle isn't jealous that Cara lets me draw on her specials board. She's busy doing what she loves best—searching for loose change. People sometimes drop coins by the food truck window. Turtle was rooting round in the sand under the counter.

"I found one quarter and a dime!" she yells.

Mom goes to her studio to do some more work. Dad, Turtle, and I keep with our library plan. We pass Happy Trails Markct, Hiking Outfitters, and Tres Café—Mom's favorite coffee shop. We're so busy looking in the window of the coffee shop to see if there's anyone we know, we nearly trip over a woman placing a large sign on the sidewalk in front of the old bank building.

Turtle backs up to see what the sign says. She's been practicing her reading with Bo, the Great Dane who used to belong to my family (well, sort of). We gave Bo to our school as a reading dog, and he sometimes comes over to our house for slumber parties. Because of Bo, Turtle now wants to sound out everything.

"'Toy store coming soon!'" she reads. She looks at me and Dad to make sure she got it right.

I nod with my mouth wide open. Not because Turtle can read these words. But hey—a toy store! If Cara can't have a restaurant in this building, a toy store is the next best thing!

"Why hello!" the woman says directly to Turtle and me. She's dressed kind of like a fairy godmother.

"What are your names?"

"I'm Turtle and this is Twig," my sister says.

"Pardon me?"

I repeat our names slowly.

"Turtle and Twig?" says the woman. "What charming nicknames."

"Those are our real names," I tell her. I have to tell grown-ups this a lot. Here's how you know if they don't believe you:

- They tilt their head and make their mouth into a straight line.

• If they really don't believe you, they close one
  eye.

"My mom and dad liked those names," I say.

"Why you poor things," the woman says to us (but
looking at my dad). "Imagine being named after a
stick and a reptile."

What? I want to tell her that I love my name! That
it reminds me of trees that bend, and nests that hold
eggs, and birds that sing. I look to my dad for help.

"Their names are simple and unique," Dad says
calmly. He doesn't worry much about what others
think. But I do. And Turtle does even more.

"Turtle is a pretty name!" she says. "Besides,
turtles have hard shells and so do I!"

Mom helped her come up with that answer the
first time she was teased. Now she says that to
everyone.

The only thing Turtle doesn't like about her name
is that people give her turtles all the time. On her
birthday, she gets turtle books, turtle games, stuffed
turtles, even bobblehead turtles. When we moved
to our tiny house, she left every one of her turtles
behind.

Nobody gives me twigs.

"I see," says the woman. "Well, my name is Mrs.
Wallaby and I hope you'll come visit the toy store
when we have our grand opening next week."

(I want to say, *Wallaby, like the rodent?* But I

don't. Partly because I'm not sure if wallabies are rodents and partly because I don't want to be mean like this fairy godmother who is not really like a fairy godmother at all.)

"What's the name of your store?" Dad asks.

Mrs. Wallaby huffs. "I haven't been able to decide," she says. "But I'm going to have a contest! Children will have a chance to submit a name. The winner will get to choose a toy from the store. See?

I've put the rules right here in the window."

"Any toy?" I ask, for once beating Turtle to the question.

"Any toy under fifty dollars!" she says.

Turtle and I grab hands and jump up and down.

"Good luck!" says Mrs. Wallaby as we say our goodbyes and head to the library.

"We should start thinking of names for the toy store right now!" Turtle says.

I agree. Given Mrs. Wallaby's reaction to our names, coming up with one for her store isn't going to be easy.

CHAPTER 2

I'm sitting on a beanbag chair in Mom and Dad's studio, which used to be an empty storage room in the back of Mr. Sudsy's laundromat. Mr. Sudsy (whose real name is Mr. Bryant) is our other next-door neighbor. He lives in the apartment above the laundromat.

My new stack of library books is beside me, but I'm way too distracted to read. I'm trying to think of the perfect name for Mrs. Wallaby's toy store. I imagine Mrs. Wallaby making an announcement:

And the winner is . . . Twig McKay! I imagine my clever store name printed on the sign out front. Most of all, I imagine myself walking up and down the aisles, looking at all the toys, knowing I can have any one I want.

So far, I've come up with Toy Treasures and Toyland, but both are names of stores back in Boston where we used to live . . . and probably names that Mrs. Wallaby has thought of already.

Speaking of Mrs. Wallaby . . . I pull out the book on wallabies from the stack of library books

beside me. I can tell by the picture on the cover that wallabies are not rodents—they look like little kangaroos. But which family do they belong to? I open the book and discover that wallabies are marsupials—mammals that carry their babies in pouches. Cute.

"Stop reading!" Turtle says. "There are new clothes in the lost and found!"

I look up. Turtle's wearing a man's plaid flannel shirt that goes down to her knees.

"Come on," she says, coaxing me with her hands. "You know you want to!"

I have to admit, exploring the lost-and-found box is fun. I pull myself up.

"I'm heading out on the road," Turtle says in a deep grown-up voiceas she finishes fastening the buttons.

"I've got a three-day trip ahead."

19

"Trucker?" I ask, picking out a sweater that's been all stretched out by the washer. Whoever left this probably left it on purpose.

Turtle nods. No surprise. Playing with miniature cars and trucks with her best buddy, Jordan, is her latest obsession. "What are you going to be?" she asks.

The long drooping sleeves on this abandoned sweater remind me of snakes. I pull them up over my wrists. "A zookeeper," I say.

"Well, Ms. Zookeeper," she says, "I've got five loads of bananas in the back of my truck for your monkeys."

Mr. Bryant looks up from his folding and smiles.

"Monkeys shouldn't eat bananas that don't grow in the wild," I tell her. "They're too sweet." I read that in a library book just last week.

"Well then, you'll just have to feed them to the people who come to the zoo," she says.

I laugh and pretend to give everyone who comes through my imaginary zoo gate a free banana. I'm acting like a total banana maniac when a couple comes through the door carrying two large laundry baskets.

Even though they grin when they see us, Turtle and I instantly scoot back into the studio where Mom is staring at her computer screen.

"If I win the toy store contest," Turtle says, plunking down on the beanbag, "I'm going to choose a Hot Rider eighteen-wheel truck. Just like the one Jordan got for her birthday."

"Don't forget," Mom says. "Every time a new toy comes into our tiny house, an old toy must go out."

"I know," Turtle says. "Five toys only. But this

will be part of my truck collection."

"Then another truck in your collection will have

to go," Mom says. "We agreed."

Sigh. I'd hoped Mom would forget about that rule.

Back in Boston, I had my own room and shelves full

of toys. Choosing just five to bring was crazy hard.

Here's what happened when Mom saw everything I

planned on packing for the move:

Mom: "Wait, wait, wait! That's way more than five toys!"

Me: "The microscope and inventor's kit and the baking oven aren't really toys. They're educational."

Mom: Tilts her head.

Me: "And the five ceramic skunks aren't five toys. They're one collection."

Mom: Closes one eye and points to another pile.

Me: "Craft supplies."

Mom: "And I suppose these stuffed animals are a collection of friends?"

Me: "Exactly. Besides they can go on my bed."

Mom: "This isn't going to work, Twig. Let's agree to this: You may choose four favorite objects and one collection. But your collection may not have more than five things."

That's when I'd collapsed on the floor. "That's impossible!" I had said.

Mom had sat down on the carpet with me. "You're a problem solver, Twig. What's making this so hard?"

I wasn't sure I wanted to tell her. "I have to bring the things that I talk to," I whispered, thinking that I was not acting like a third-grader.

"Like your Universe Dolls?" she'd asked.

I shook my head. I didn't talk to my Universe Dolls. They just talked to each other.

"Like Flat Bear," I'd said. Flat Bear is a plushy bag that when stuffed with my pajamas looked like a bear head. Only, I never remembered to keep my pajamas inside. So, he became known as Flat Bear and he was a great listener. "I can't hurt his feelings by giving him away."

24

Mom reminded me that my things would proba-bly find another kid who would love them, but that didn't make things much easier. Here are the things I finally packed:

- Flat Bear
- Snow Puff (my beanbag kitten)
- A folding pet store (with little animals, so it's kind of a sneaky collection)

- Monopoly (another sneaky collection, because the game pieces are like a little family to me)
- My porcelain Mama Skunk and her four adorable babies (my true collection)

The feelings from that day, when I had to choose five toys, were coming back to me now. I wanted to be the one to come up with a catchy title for Mrs. Wallaby's store. I wanted to win the prize. But which of my toys could I give up?

CHAPTER 3

The next day, Dad gets a text from Angela's mom.
(Angela is my BFF.) Angela wants me to come over
and play after lunch. Our friend David is coming too.

Yes! I love visiting Angela's house, which is a
lodge up on one of the mountainsides in Happy
Trails.

"She says to bring your Universe Dolls," says Dad.
He scrunches his face to show me that he knows
this is a problem.

I gave my Universe Dolls to the homeless shelter

in Boston before we left. Universe Dolls are action figures that look like people—until you move their parts around. Then they transform into natural things like animals or lightning. Everybody plays with them.

"I'll tell her mom that you don't own them any longer," he says while tapping away on his tablet.

I close my library book and think about the ones I used to own: Olivia, who morphed into a snowy owl; Jag, who morphed into a jaguar; and Willow, who morphed into wind. Suddenly, I miss them.

"Angela's mom says that Angela will be happy to share."

"See, Twigster?" Mom says, sitting down on the couch next to me. "Sharing's another way of enjoying yourself without owning lots of things."

Turtle looks up from where she's playing with her

trucks on the floor. She gives me an understanding look that says, *Sure, but sometimes you just want stuff.* Right now, I was feeling a big old mountain of want.

On the drive to Angela's house, I think about telling my friends about Mrs. Wallaby's naming contest. I can just picture their happy faces. But then I reconsider.

If I tell them about the contest, there will be more competition for Turtle and me. Telling them doesn't feel fair to my sister. I decide not to say anything.

Mom says hello to Mrs. Lewis, and I head straight to Angela's room.

"I am the Keeper of the Oceans! Welcome!" says Angela as I appear in the doorway. She's holding out Dalia, who morphs into a sleek dolphin. David is sitting next to her, holding Elana (who morphs into an eagle) and Flynn (who morphs into a fox). In front of them is the Universe Dolls underwater cave and the Sky Cloud restaurant. There are lots of other dolls scattered about.

"Wow!" I say. "You guys sure have a lot of

Universe Dolls!" I bend down and peek into the underwater cave. It's got bunk beds made out of pretend driftwood, and a table and chairs made out of pretend seashells.

"Where are your Universe Dolls?" David asks.

"She doesn't have any," Angela says. "There isn't room in her tiny house. . . . So, we can share," she adds.

I look at Elana, transformed into an eagle in David's left hand. For some reason, I've always liked the dolls that can fly best. Probably because of my tree-like name.

David sees me looking at Elana and tightens his grip. Then he quickly scans the floor. He drops Flynn and picks up Stella, who morphs into a shooting star. "Here," he says. "You can play with her. She was my cousin's."

I look down at Stella, who has only a few strands of blond hair coming out of her head. Her cheek has a black ink smudge on it and she's missing one hand. I doubt she'll look much brighter transformed into a star.

Maybe I don't look too thrilled, because David's kindness comes out and he offers me Wanda (transformed as a wolf) too. Wanda looks fierce.

"And you can have Mikah, who turns into a mustang," says Angela, handing me one of her dolls.

I look down at Stella again as I speak to her in my head. *I think you are beautiful, Stella*, I tell her. And the weird thing is, I really do.

Thank you, she says to me in a twinkly voice. I

swear her eyes sparkle.

"Do you want more than three dolls?" Angela asks.

I look up from Stella and see that they're still holding out Wanda and Mikah.

"I'm good with Stella," I say. "I don't need any other dolls."

"Are you sure?" asks Angela. "Stella looks like she's lost more battles than she's won."

"You won't have as much fun with just one doll," David says.

"Sure I will," I say. "Stella can do amazing things."

And she does. Stella shines light into the cave and toasts marshmallows at the Sky Cloud restaurant— after she saves the world from darkness, that is.

"I want to buy the Universe Doll underground camp," David says, while we're lying on the floor

munching the popcorn that Angela's mother popped
for us. "It has cool gear."

"I bet it's really expensive," Angela says.

I imagine little pop-up tents and a fire circle.
"Hey! Did you know—"

I don't finish my sentence. I want to tell them
about the naming contest so badly. But the more
people I tell, the less chance I have of winning.

I stuff my mouth with a big handful of popcorn
instead.

34

"Do we know what?" David asks.

I think fast. "Do you know—"

Popcorn comes flying out of my mouth. David and Angela laugh. Then I laugh, then they laugh again. Everyone forgets that I had something to say.

If I win, I tell myself, *I'll pick the underground camp and share.*

We play a little while longer, then Mom arrives to take me home.

As I reach for the car door, David and Angela come running out.

"You can keep Stella," David says, holding her out to me. "I don't want her anymore."

I'm about to say *No thank you, I'm not ready to give up one of my old toys yet,* but Stella looks so cute.

And she seems to want to come home with me.

I look up at my mom, who is still standing on the steps talking to Angela's mom. "Thank you, David," I say and tuck Stella into my pocket.

Angela smiles and bounces on her feet.

I can't help myself. I love my friends. My news rushes out. "The new toy store in town is having a naming contest and the winner gets to pick any toy in the store!"

"Really?" says Angela. "A new toy store? A contest?!"

"Any toy?" David asks. "I'm going to make a

whole list of names and choose the best one!"

"Me too!" says Angela. "And I'm going to ask my mom to help. She helps businesses come up with names."

I feel bad that Turtle and my chances are going down. "Let's try to keep the contest to ourselves," I say.

Angela and David look at each other. David shrugs.

"Okay," says Angela.

When we drive off, I'm feeling happy/scared.

Happy that I have such good friends.

Happy that I have a new toy in my pocket.

Scared that Mom will find out and I will have to give something up.

CHAPTER 4

When I arrive home, Turtle is sitting at our little fold-up table. "I found three dimes and a penny in the dryers at Sudsy's!" she tells me. That girl is always finding money. She says if I stopped looking up at the trees all the time, I'd find more too.

Without thinking, my hand goes to my pocket.

Turtle looks.

"What's in there?" she asks.

For a moment, I think of giving her a peek at my new doll (which isn't very new). But she'd ask me which toy I'm giving up and I'm not ready to have that conversation. I don't even like thinking about it.

"A tissue," I say, which is a really lame answer because anyone looking at my pocket can see a sharp edge . . . and tissues don't have sharp edges.

Fortunately, she turns back to her counting.

I leave her, and my mom and dad who have begun to cook dinner, and climb the narrow stairs up to our loft.

I plop down on my sleeping bag and pull out Stella. *Oooh, is this where I live now?* I imagine her saying. The smudge on her cheek looks like a worm tattoo. I decide it's an inchworm.

Inchworms are so cute when they stand up and look around.

Flat Bear is sitting (if a flat pajama-bag head can sit) on my pillow. I introduce Stella to him. I can tell

immediately that he's happy to have a new friend.
But then I think of him worried, wondering, *Are you
going to give me away, Twig? Am I the one who
has to go?*

I glance over at my shelf, and Snow Puff, the five
skunks, my Monopoly game, and the little pet shop
all seem to be asking me the same thing: *Which one
of us has to go?*

I shake my head. I'm eight. I know that things don't talk, that they don't have feelings. *It's just your imagination, Twig,* I say to myself, and even though I know that it's a hundred percent true, I still feel bad.

I lie down on my sleeping bag for a few moments listening to the sounds below. Mom and Dad are pulling out the ingredients to make enchiladas while Turtle is singing to herself. I peek up through the skylight and think of toy store names.

Toy Tower (not very fitting)

Toy Palace (same)

Terrific Toys (maybe?)

The Toybox (I like this one! The building is sort of boxy.)

I love playing with words. Words that begin with a *T* make you pay attention. Like if you say *tree,*

tree, tree quickly, you sound like a bird chirping. I like that both my name and my sister's begin with *T*s.

Coming up with two good names for a toy store gives me a brilliant idea. Turtle and I should come up with lots of names together. Then we can choose the two best, and if one of them wins, we can share the prize!

Maybe, just maybe, if we won a toy to share, Mom and Dad won't make us give something up.

"Hey Turtle," I call out to my sister in the room below. That's a cool thing about a tiny house. You don't have to move to talk to someone. Everyone can hear you.

"Do you want to come up with the two best names for the toy store contest together, and if we win, we'll share the prize?"

She looks up from her counting for a second. "Nah," she says. "I want a truck and I want it all to myself."

"Greedy one," I say kiddingly. "If your name for the store isn't selected, you won't win anything at all."

"That's okay," she says. "I have enough money now to buy a truck. And as soon as the toy store opens, that's what I'm going to do!"

I sigh and look at Stella. I imagine all the fun I could have with the underground camp. I could invite Angela and David over, and they'd bring all their Universe Dolls.

I'll see my magical friends again! I imagine Stella saying.

Flat Bear stares at me with what looks like fear in his eyes, and I think that he must be really good

44

at counting. Keeping Stella and winning a new toy would mean two old toys would have to go.

"Don't worry," I whisper to all my toys in the loft. "I have two goals. To win the contest . . ."

You can do it! I hear Stella telling me. *You're good with words!*

"And to convince Mom and Dad to let us keep more than five toys."

Flat Bear flattens (even more) . . . with relief.

CHAPTER 5

The next morning, I put on the same jeans that I wore over the weekend. (My other pants are pocketless.)

"It's laundry day," Dad says. "Don't you want those washed?"

"They're still good!" I say, even though they have some small grease stains from the buttered popcorn I ate (and spat out) at Angela's yesterday.

I have to wear those jeans because I need a pocket —a pocket for hiding Stella. I thought of leaving her at home. I could tuck her into my sleeping bag, but

sometimes Dad washes our bags

while we're at school. I could

leave her hidden on

my toy shelf, but

Mom's been taking

random pictures of our

tiny house. Today might

be the day she decides

to rearrange our loft.

So, even though

Happy Trails Elementary has a

"no toys" rule, I tuck Stella into my pocket.

"I can't wait to buy my new truck," Turtle says on

the way to school.

I look up at the mountain ahead of us. "Do you

know which toy you'll give away?" I ask.

"Yup!" she says. "My light-up unicorn."

An older boy nearly bumps into me as I stop smack in the middle of the sidewalk. "Really?"

"Keep walking!" Turtle says to me. "I don't want to be late."

"But you love your unicorn!"

"I loved it when I was five. Now I'm six."

Things seem to come so easily to Turtle.

"But what if we could convince Mom and Dad to let us have more than five toys?" I ask.

"You already tried that in Boston," Twig reminds me.

It's true. "Living in a tiny house means being intentional," Dad had said.

Being intentional means choosing to be your best self. But maybe my best self can intentionally change my parents' mind. I look down at my T-shirt.

I wish I'd worn my Determined Squirrel T-shirt.

"I've got to think of something," I tell my sister.

❧

When Turtle and I arrive at school, Angela and David are surrounded by kids on the playground— and they're all talking about the toy store naming contest.

I can't believe it! They promised that it would be our secret. Now everyone will enter!

"Each person can only submit one idea," says David.

"I'm going to have my parents and my cat submit a name," Piper says. "And if they win, they'll give the toy to me."

"Cats don't count," I say, joining the group. "And neither do parents. Only children. It's in the rules." I hope that David and Angela pick up on my frustration.

"My baby brother is a child," says Janelle. "But if I

used his name and he won, my parents would probably

allow me to choose the toy and keep it."

By the time the bell rings for us to go into school, it seems that every kid on the playground is planning on entering one or more names. That's more than thirty ideas!

Why did I spill the beans? I huff my way into line.

"I didn't tell them about the contest," Angela says as she and David catch up to me.

"Me either," says David. "They saw the same sign on Main Street that you did."

Of course, the sign. Did I really think that others wouldn't see it too?

"It was silly to think that the news wouldn't get around," I say to my friends.

The recess monitor puts her fingers to her lips, reminding us that we have to be quiet in the halls.

Mr. Harbor invites us to the carpet for Morning Meeting and asks us to put our thoughts of the contest aside until the next recess. Then he reminds us that it's our class's turn to read to Bo in the library. "And, Twig," he says, "it's your turn to go first."

"Really?" I ask, popping up on my knees.

He smiles. "Really."

Who cares about an old contest! I grab my latest Frankie Sparks book and do my fastest speed-walking, hoping to get as many minutes as possible with my pal Bo.

I wave to our librarian, Mr. Lucas, and head over to the reading corner where Bo is waiting for me.

I still expect him to jump up into my arms when he sees me (like he did when he lived with my grandma). But now that he's been trained as a reading dog, Bo

sits as still as he can, and waits for me to come to
him. Good dog, Bo!

I can tell by the smile on his face and the extra
wags in this tail that he still loves, loves, loves me.
We exchange kisses and then we both stretch out on
the floor. I place my head on Bo's belly and begin to
read.

But even though Frankie Spark books are really
good, I don't get far into the story. I'm too distracted
by the slightly pointy, sharp lump in my pocket.

"Can you keep a secret?" I ask Bo. I know he can,

so I don't wait for him to give me a sign.

"Look," I say, pulling Stella out of my pocket. "David gave her to me."

Bo gives Stella a big old lick, which makes me giggle. I hope she still has some hair left.

Then I look up and see Mr. Lucas looking at me.

Oh, no! I completely forgot where I was!

He gets up from his chair and heads in my direction.

I quickly squeeze Stella back into my pocket.

Bending down, Mr. Lucas asks, "Twig, are you feeding Bo?"

I quickly shake my head no.

"Since Bo used to belong to your grandma, I know that it must be awfully tempting to feed him treats."

"I wasn't. Really! Bo would get sick if everyone fed him," I say, showing that I remember the reading

Dog Rules. "I would hate for Bo to get sick."

"Okay," says Mr. Lucas. "I just want to make sure. I'm sorry. My mistake."

He looks genuinely sorry and I feel bad. I didn't lie about feeding Bo, but I didn't exactly tell the truth either.

I can see a little bit of Bo drool soaking through my pants pocket.

Fortunately, no one else notices the drool—or the guilt on my face.

Not even Turtle when she meets me at the end of the day.

It's not like her to not notice things.

"What's wrong?" I ask.

"Everyone's entering the naming contest," she says.

I sigh. "I know," I say. "It seems like our chances of winning are getting slimmer and slimmer."

"Worse," Turtle says. "When I told some kids on the playground that I was going to choose a miniature truck if I won, they made fun of me."

"Why?" I ask. "Did they think you should choose

something bigger? Something more expensive?"

Again, she shakes her head. "They said trucks are for boys."

I hear Mom's voice in my head: *That's ridiculous!* "What did you say?" I ask, sounding just like her.

"I said that trucks are for everyone. That my grandma has a truck."

"That's a good answer," I say. And it is. I'm not sure I would have come up with it as fast.

"Yeah, but I still felt pushed away."

I nod, knowing what she means. It's like there's some rule book somewhere that says we should all like the same things. "Have you thought of a name for the toy store?" I ask.

She nods. "You won't laugh?"

"Never," I say.

She stops and, with a sweep of her arm, says, "Abracadabra!"

I don't laugh at all.

It seems magical.

And . . . perfect.

"I think you're going to win," I tell her.

CHAPTER 6

That afternoon, David, Angela, and I have Social Skills Club with Mia and Warren. We attend once or twice a week in Ms. Lisa's room. Social Skills Club was meant to help us make friends, but we've already done that. (We don't tell our teachers though. We want to keep on being members of this club.)

Ms. Lisa has spread out a board game on the table.

"Can we think up names for the new toy store instead?" Mia asks.

Great idea! "Please?" we all say at once.

Ms. Lisa likes any activity that involves cooperation. "Okay," she says. "We'll play my game next time."

So the five of us begin brainstorming. Ms. Lisa writes our ideas down on the whiteboard.

Here's what I notice about brainstorming:

• The first ideas everyone comes up with are the obvious. All our first ideas had the word *toy* in them.

• The more ideas we come up with, the more creative our brains get.

• The very best ideas are those that all five of us tried to make better. Like these:

Warren: Toys, Toys, Toys! (okay)

Me: Land of Play (okay)

Lisa: Playland (okay)

Angela: On the Way to the Land of Play (rhyming, but too long)

David: The Magic Carpet (takes you to playland the way our rug at home does)

I convince my friends to brainstorm reasons why Mom and Dad should agree to let Turtle and me have more toys. But even though they come up with some good reasons, I can imagine my parents' response to all of them:

• Tiny spaces need to be simpler, tidier.

- The less time picking up, the more time to do things.

- When you have lots of toys, many are forgotten.

- Having fewer things makes the ones you have more special.

- There has to be a limit somewhere (if the limit was six, we'd want seven).

Still, I really want Stella and I really want to win the contest and I really *really* don't want to give anything up. It's just a fact.

As soon as I get home that afternoon, I climb up to the loft I share with Turtle, unzip Flat Bear, and tuck Stella inside. It's not a perfect hiding place, but I can't make the mistake of taking her to school again. I'm really lucky that Mr. Lucas didn't see her and take her away from me.

I hate keeping Stella a secret from my family, I think as I climb back down the stairs. I feel sneaky. Plus, I'm more of a rule follower than a rule breaker. I've got to figure something out!

I join Mom and Turtle for fruit and oatmeal cookies on the porch and hope that Mom can't read the sneakiness on my face. She's a good feelings detective.

But she has something she's eager to say. I can tell.

"Do you guys want to go on a photo shoot with me this afternoon?"

"Where to?" I ask cautiously.

I love going on photo shoots—when Mom's taking pictures of places. (Photo shoots of *people* get really boring because folks are never happy with the expressions on their faces or the way they're standing, and always want Mom to keep taking more pictures.)

Mom raises her eyebrows and gives us a big smile, as if to say, *You're going to love this one!*

"The playground?" Turtle asks.

"The library?" I ask. Sometimes Mom lets us pose in the pictures. I would love to be photographed in front of the stuffed bear they have there, reading a big fat book.

"The new toy store!" she says, tucking her toes underneath her chair so we don't step on them as we jump up and down.

Do we ever!

Mrs. Wallaby greets us at the door and invites us inside. Her hair is piled high in a bun with a sparkly headband. "Look at your shirt!" she says to Mom. "All those purple splotches on it make you look like you fell into a grape vat!"

I look at Turtle with wide eyes. Her mouth drops open. I'm remembering Mrs. Wallaby's comments about our names, and my hands clench into fists.

But Mom just laughs. "Perhaps I do," she says. "But I love this shirt. It makes me happy."

"Then you should absolutely wear it," says Mrs.

Wallaby. "Always wear what makes you happy. That's what I say!"

My hands unclench. Mom's feelings didn't get hurt. And Mrs. Wallaby changed her tune.

Turtle gives me a little shrug.

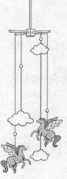

Maybe Mrs. Wallaby isn't mean. Maybe she's just very free with her opinions.

"Have a look around, girls!" she says, and then leads Mom to the back room so they can use her computer. She wants Mom to tell her what kinds of pictures on social media are the most useful.

Inside the store are dragon kites, Pegasus mobiles, and spaceships hanging from the ceiling. On the floor there is a long tube to crawl through and a train set with a little village. And in between the stuff flying from the ceiling and trailing along the floor are shelves and shelves of toys.

Turtle is racing around looking for the specific Hot Rider she wants to buy.

"Twig!" she says. "This store is so confusing!"

I turn the corner to help her. "What do you mean?"

"Well, the bulldozers and the cranes are over on this shelf, and the convertibles and the campers are on this shelf, and I can't find an eighteen-wheeler at all."

"Maybe the toys aren't really organized," I tell her. "Maybe they're just willy-nilly."

But the more I glance around, the more I realize that the toys are organized. They're organized by the color of the packaging. Blue and green packages are on one side. Pink and purple packages are on the other. The bulldozer is in a blue package. The convertible is in a pink package. I point this out to Turtle.

"It doesn't make sense!" Turtle says. "Why can't all the Hot Riders be in one place?"

I have a sneaky suspicion that Mrs. Wallaby has

decided that one side of the toy store is for girls and the other is for boys, but I don't want Turtle to feel confused and left out the way she was when the girls at school teased her for wanting a truck.

I get an idea super fast. "Let's help Mrs. Wallaby by gathering all the trucks and putting them in one place!" I say.

"Good idea, Twig!" she says to me.

But Turtle seems to need no help, so I decide to put all the Universe Dolls together. I get Flynn, who is in a blue package, and a new Stella, who is in a pink package, and put them together.

Turtle and I move quickly. We can hear Mom and Mrs. Wallaby laughing together in the back room, but we want to surprise them when Mom comes out to take pictures.

"Stop! What are you girls doing?" It's Mrs. Wallaby,

with Mom. She's standing in the doorway shocked and very unhappy to see us rearranging shelves. "It took me hours to put all of these toys in place!"

"Surprise!" I say, but it comes out wilted. (Have I turned into a total rule breaker?)

"The toys were all jumbled," Turtle says.

"They were arranged by color, which made it really hard to find anything," I add.

"Yeah!" says Turtle. She's got her hands on her hips. "There are no such things as girl toys and boy toys." I guess she figured out Mrs. Wallaby's thinking on her own.

"No. Such. Thing," I add, knowing full well that the two of us are in Very. Big. Trouble.

CHAPTER 7

For a moment, it looks as if Mom is going to smile at what we had done. But then she quickly changes course. She tells us to apologize and put the toys back in their original places. "It was not your decision to make," she says. "If you disagreed with Mrs. Wallaby's method of arranging toys, you should have talked with her—shared your opinion."

Turtle and I both say we're sorry, but I'm not sure Mrs. Wallaby hears us. She seems very frazzled. So, we quickly grab up the toys and put them back as best we can. (It's not hard, the color of the boxes guides us.)

Then Mom makes us sit on a bench near the office door while she takes pictures. She starts with the ceiling and the floor, which are the most magical and fun parts of the store. If my sister and I hadn't upset Mrs. Wallaby, Mom would be taking our pictures emerging from the tunnel or looking up at the winged horses. Sitting here is our punishment.

When Mom starts to photograph the shelves, Mrs. Wallaby stops her.

"Would you mind, Chloe," she says to Mom, "if we took the rest of the pictures in a day or two?"

Mom brings the camera away from her face. "So close to the opening?"

Mrs. Wallaby nods.

"If that's what you want to do," Mom says, "of

course." She gives us a hand signal that tells us to pop up and join her.

"I want to think about what the girls said," Mrs. Wallaby explains. "After all, they are my customers."

"We'll be your best customers!" Turtle says.

"We can help you switch things around if you want," I say, hoping that I'm not being disrespectful. "We've had plenty of practice in moving."

"Thank you," says Mrs. Wallaby. "But I'm not sure I can think of a better way to display the toys."

After dinner, we hang out in the studio. Turtle doesn't want to play Dress-up. Instead, she wants to draw her ideas for organizing the store. I might be good at drawing carrot tops, but Turtle is superbly good at drawing maps.

"This area has toys for makers," she says. "Like Legos, sewing kits, robot-building kits, cooking ovens, and model rockets."

"What are these toys?" I ask, pointing to another section of her map.

"Those are toys for explorers."

"Like binoculars?" I ask.

She nods. "And walkie-talkies, and butterfly kits."

Together we come up with some more organizing ideas: toys for scientists, toys for active kids.

Mom and Dad come over to see our work.

"I'm impressed," says Mom. "But I wonder if other kids will know where to look in the store."

"Mrs. Wallaby can hang signs!" I say.

"Hmmmm." That's Dad's thinking sound. "Maybe I could offer to draw some for Mrs. Wallaby," he says.

"Great idea!" says Turtle. "You could draw kids playing with the toys on the signs to help people understand the words!"

"That's if Mrs. Wallaby's interested," says Dad. "Just because we like these ideas, doesn't mean she's on board. After all, it is her store."

Turtle turns to Mom. "Will you give her my map?" she asks. "Tomorrow? So she has time to think?"

Mom looks at Dad who looks back at Mom. "Okay," she says. You can tell that it makes her nervous. After all, Mrs. Wallaby hired Mom to take pictures. She's Mom's boss.

Before Turtle hands Mom the map, she asks me to write some words at the top.

"You can sound them out," I encourage her.

"Not this time," says Turtle. "I don't think Mrs. Wallaby reads first-grade spelling."

"Maybe you're right."

She hands me a small slip of paper and tells me what to write.

MRS. WALLABY'S TOY STORE

by Turtle McKay

CHAPTER 8

After school the next day, Turtle and I race home. We can't wait to hear what Mrs. Wallaby said about Turtle's toy store ideas.

Mom and Dad are sitting on the couch, looking at his comics on his tablet.

"Did Mrs. Wallaby like our plan?" Turtle asks.

Mom and Dad look up and smile. "Yes," Mom says slowly. You can tell there's a *no* coming too.

"She liked the idea of sorting the toys in more interesting ways. But she wants to come up with her own categories."

Turtle makes a pouty face.

"Does she want our help moving things?" I ask as I put my backpack in my cupboard under the stairs.

"No. She says to thank you, but she wants to think about the categories as she moves things around."

That makes sense, I think. Lots of toys can go in more than one place. Like a terrarium kit. It could go in the maker section, the explorer section, or the section for scientists.

"So now we just wait and see?" asks Turtle, who has plopped onto the floor. She's using her backpack to lean on.

Dad changes the subject. "We thought we might take a trip to the Vintage Store today," he says. The Vintage Store is where you can buy, sell, or trade used things. There's a little of everything: furniture, clothes, kitchenwares, toys, and books. Dad wants to trade a short-sleeved shirt for one with long sleeves. Mom decides to sell two large pots we brought from Boston. "We just don't have enough room in these cupboards," she says.

"I'll sell my light-up unicorn," Turtle says, "so I can buy my new truck!"

My stomach drops. I still haven't figured out how to tell my parents about Stella without giving something up.

Stella. I decide to retrieve her from her hiding place in Flat Bear. I tuck her into my front pocket and join my family as they're heading out the door.

"Everything okay?" Mom asks as we walk along Main Street. She knows that I typically love going to the Vintage Store. You never know what you're going to see.

I try to smile and nod, not ready to tell her about the problem I'm grappling with. Not when Turtle is so bravely handing over her formerly prized possession.

We enter the store and Turtle walks right up to Georgia, the store owner, and tells her, "I'd like to sell this light-up unicorn, please."

While Georgia tells Turtle how much she'll pay for her unicorn, Mom and Dad slide over to the music section. Even though my parents sold their record player, they still like looking at the old records. Mom sets the pots that she brought to sell down at her feet while she flips through them.

I decide to check out the toy shelves before heading over to the book section.

There are some coloring books with only the first

pages filled in. We never buy those 'cause Dad just draws us coloring pages. There's also a Monopoly game like mine. I wonder if the Vintage Store will take a game if they already have the same one. (That is, if that's what I choose to give up. I imagine Thimble whispering, *But I love sitting on your finger!* and shake the thought from my head.) I start to look at electronic toys when something catches my eye.

"Turtle, there's a little truck here."

Turtle says "Excuse me" to Georgia, who is brushing the mane on the light-up unicorn.

"Hey, what's that sticking out of your pocket?"

she asks me as she walks over.

I look down. Stella has one leg poking out.

"I'll tell you later," I whisper.

"Did you take something?" she asks, way too loudly. "Are you stealing?"

NO! I mouth. I grab Turtle's arm and pull her in closer. I open the top of my pocket and show her Stella. Then I whisper, "David gave her to me the day I played at Angela's. I couldn't show you because then I'd have to choose a toy to give up. And I don't know how to do that."

Here's how you know if someone is trying to decide if they can believe you:

- They squint their eyes.
- They tilt their head to one side.
- They move their lips over to one side of their mouth.

"I would never steal," I say, hoping she won't make a scene.

Turtle's convinced. "I won't tell Mom and Dad,"

she says, looking over the truck on the shelf.

"Thanks," I say, breathing easier.

"But you should."

She's right. I've got to tell them.

I decide to do it right now.

I'm tired of trying to keep Stella a secret.

I find my parents in the corner, looking at guitars. "Can I talk to you guys for a moment?"

"Of course," says Dad, still staring at a twelve-string he'd love to own.

"Can we go outside?" I say. "I want to talk privately."

Mom looks surprised, but she picks up the pots that are still on the floor by the records and all four of us head out to the sidewalk.

"We'll be right back!" Dad calls to Georgia.

"I have to show you something," I say, as I pull Stella from my pocket.

86

Turtle takes her from me so she can transform

her into a star.

"Where did *she* come from?" Mom asks.

"David gave her to me when I played at Angela's,"

I repeat. "And I've been keeping her a secret because

I don't want to give one of my other toys away."

"Oh, Twigster," says Mom. She hands Dad the pots and pulls me in for a hug. "Letting go is hard."

"But do we have to do so much letting go?" I ask. "Can't we work out a new system of counting toys? Sometimes people give you presents, sometimes you win contests. Something bad shouldn't have to happen every time something good does."

Mom and Dad look at each other and I can tell that they get what I'm saying.

"I just want to be happy to have Stella," I say, as Twig hands her back to me.

"You make a good point," Dad says.

"Then can we have six toys? Or seven?" Turtle asks.

"I don't think that's the solution," Mom says, reaching for the pots again. "But we can figure this out."

The pots! They give me a great brainstorm!

"I've got it!" I say. "Don't sell the cooking pots. We can put our games and puzzles on the first two shelves in our room, and the pots on the top. Turtle and I can each have one potful of toys. That will keep our toys contained, and we won't have to give something away unless our pot is spilling over."

Turtle jumps up and down. "And you can keep your pots! I call the smaller one!" she says.

I look at Turtle to see if she means it. "You can't hold as many toys in the smaller pot," I say.

"But I can carry it downstairs with me. That will make picking it up much easier! Besides, I can fit a lot of small trucks in this pot," she says, taking the small one out of Mom's hands.

"It's a creative solution," says Dad. "And it does use our old things in new ways."

Mom likes both those things. "Good solution!" Mom says. "Let's try it."

We head back into the store. Mom tells Georgia that they won't be selling the pots after all.

"May I have my unicorn back for a moment?" Turtle asks.

Georgia hands it to her.

Turtle places it in the small pot. It fits with room around the edges for vehicles! "I think I'll keep her," she says.

"So, does that mean you won't be selling anything today?" ask Georgia.

"Just one trade," says Dad, holding up his short-sleeved shirt.

"Come help me pick out a new one, girls," he

says, but I can't really concentrate.

I stand nearby and smile. And smile, and smile, and smile.

Mom and Dad really liked my idea!

And I get to keep Stella.

CHAPTER 9

Finally, the day of the grand opening of the toy store arrives!

"Wait!" I shout as Turtle and I leave for school. "We haven't placed our entries in the box!"

We'd spent so much time thinking about the organization of the toy store, we almost forgot to enter the contest. Each toy store name had to be printed on a slip of paper with the entrant's name (*entrant* just means the person who's entering the contest) and dropped in the box at the toy store by noon.

"I'll take them this morning," Dad says. "I have to visit the store one more time to hang the signs anyway."

Phew! "They're in the studio," I say. "Mine says Pocketful of Toys!" I got the idea for this name from looking at the book about wallabies.

"Come on, Twig!" says Turtle. "Dad will find them." She hates to be late for anything.

The opening is all anyone can talk about at school. It's like a holiday. Cara is going to bring her famous carrot cupcakes and carrot cannolis for dessert. Georgia is raffling off coupons for free items at the Vintage Store. And Mr. Bryant from Sudsy's has donated money for stickers for every kid who attends the opening. That way, everyone gets a prize!

According to Angela, the doors open at four o'clock, and the name of the store will be announced at four thirty.

"I wonder what it will look like inside," David says. Then, remembering what I told him before, he adds, "Besides the flying horses and kites and the train."

I wonder what it will look like too. Mrs. Wallaby took Dad up on his offer to make signs, but he wouldn't tell us what was on them. Then Mom took pictures of the toys on the shelves, but she wouldn't let us have a sneak peek.

Warren reminds everyone that the winner can choose any toy under fifty dollars before the store closes, but no one really needs reminding.

"Is it time to go to the toy store yet?" Turtle asks

the moment we get home from school.

It's not. We have to wait forty minutes. Forty minutes is a terrible amount of time to wait. It's way more time than it takes to eat a snack, and way too little time to set up and play Magic Woods.

Dad suggests we play one game of Crazy Eights, and that helps.

When forty minutes has finally passed, Turtle practically drags us down the street. There are lots of other families arriving from every direction.

Dad makes a sweeping gesture as he opens the door, and says, "Ta-da!"

I instantly look up and recognize Dad's lettering and artwork.

The signs read:

Imagine!

Investigate!

Get Outside!

Compete!

Make Something Wonderful!

They are sort of like our ideas and sort of different.

"I like them!" Turtle says, looking up. We find both the Hot Riders and the Universe Dolls on the shelves under the *Imagine!* sign.

"What do you think?" Mrs. Wallaby says as she comes up and puts her arms around us both.

"I think the way you organized the toys is cool!" I say.

"I have you to thank," she says. "You made this store more inviting."

We did, I think. We really did.

I meet up with Angela, David, and Warren. Turtle says she's going to get in line to buy her new truck.

"Don't you want to wait to see if you won the contest?" I ask her.

"Nah. I can pay for my truck. If I win the contest, I'll get something bigger!"

She's pretty smart.

The rest of us get our free stickers from Mr. Bryant.

Finally, Mrs. Wallaby is ready to make the announcement about the store name.

All of us kids clump together in front of her.

"Happy Trails is such a wonderfully creative town!" she says. "There were so many delightful entries."

"Plenty of Play," whispers Warren.

"Joy Box!" Angela whispers.

"Pocketful of Toys," I whisper.

"Leap Frog," David whispers.

"Leap Frog?" I ask.

"It just sounds fun to me," he says, shrugging.

"Abracadabra!" says Turtle.

Mrs. Wallaby picks up the piece of paper with the winning name. She slides her glasses farther up her nose, and says, "The winner of the contest . . . the new name of this enterprise is . . .

"Mrs. Wallaby's Toy Store!"

Huh? We all look at one another, trying to figure out who suggested that name.

Then the grown-ups in the back of the room begin to clap. We kids join in.

I'm reminded of the first day when Mrs. Wallaby

commented on my sister's and my names. We should have remembered that Mrs. Wallaby likes usual, ordinary names.

"Who picked it?" asked David. "Who is the winner?"

"Oh," says Mrs. Wallaby, adjusting her glasses again and staring closely at the little slip of paper in her hands.

"Turtle McKay!"

"Turtle?"

Everyone claps again. This time, more loudly. Some people even cheer. Especially Dad.

Turtle looks totally confused.

Mom comes up and puts her hands on her shoulder. "I thought you picked Abracadabra?" she says.

"I did," Turtle whispers.

"May we see the slip?" asks Mom. We can tell she wants the rightful entrant to win.

Mrs. Wallaby is only half listening. She hands it to Mom and goes back to the cash register where kids are standing in line to purchase toys.

Dad comes up beside us and peers at the slip over Mom's shoulder.

"Isn't this your entry?" he asks Turtle. "I found it in the studio where you said it would be."

I look over and laugh. "That's wasn't Turtle's entry, Dad. That was the title of her map!"

I grab a carrot cupcake and tell everyone over and over again how Turtle won. All the kids agree that it's a great story.

It takes Turtle a long time to choose her toy. Most of the families have left.

"Mom and Dad say you have to make a decision," I say, joining her under the *Compete!* sign.

Finally, she picks a game called Too Many Acorns!

It's not at all what I expected. "Why are you picking that?" I ask. "Why not a garage for all your trucks?" "Look," she says, pointing at the box. "It has a big tree with a secret door. It will be perfect for playing Magic Woods!"

She's right. I can picture her plastic elephant and my skunk family hiding in this tree.

"We can use the acorns for money!" she says. It sounds like so much fun. I can't wait to play!

That night, Turtle goes right to sleep. I guess winning a contest takes a lot out of you. After she selected her prize, she posed for pictures with Mrs. Wallaby.

I look up at the skylight and think about this past

week of toy store trouble. I didn't win the contest. I didn't get my clever name on the sign. I didn't win the underground camp. I didn't even win a coupon for a free item at the Vintage Store.

But I got a free sticker. Win!

I got to eat two of Cara's cupcakes. Win!

I got to play Universe Dolls with my new friends. Win!

I came up with a new idea for keeping toys. Win! Win!

I helped organize a new toy store! Win! Win!

I didn't have to give any of my toys away. Win! Win!

And tomorrow, Turtle and I will play Magic Woods with her new game. Win! Win! Win!

I hold Stella in one hand and snuggle up to Flat Bear.

Guess I'm one of the winningest girls I know.

Don't miss more
Twig and Turtle Adventures in

ABOUT THE AUTHOR

JENNIFER RICHARD JACOBSON is the award-winning author of many books for children and young adults, including the Andy Shane early-reader series and her most recent book, *The Dollar Kids*. A graduate of Harvard Graduate School of Education, when not writing, Jennifer provides trainings in Writer's Workshop for teachers. Jennifer lives in Maine with her husband and dog.